A HEART LIKE RINGO STARR

Linda Oatman High

SADDLEBACK
EDUCATIONAL PUBLISHING

GRAVEL ROAD

Bi-Normal
Edge of Ready
Falling Out of Place
A Heart Like Ringo Starr *(verse)*
I'm Just Me
Otherwise *(verse)*
Screaming Quietly
Self. Destructed.
Teeny Little Grief Machines *(verse)*
2 Days
Unchained
Varsity 170

SADDLEBACK
EDUCATIONAL PUBLISHING
www.sdlback.com

ISBN-13: 978-1-62250-968-3
ISBN-10: 1-62250-968-4
eBook: 978-1-63078-283-2

Printed in Guangzhou, China
NOR/0115/CA21401970

19 18 17 16 15   1 2 3 4 5

Dedication

For my sons, whom I carried beneath my heart, as well as for the Grand Ones, who carry around pieces of my heart.

Part 1:

ON THE LIST

Names Don't Change a Thing

Faith.
Faith Hope Stevens, 17,
destined for heaven.
That's me.

They named me Faith
so they could keep
believing.

They named me Hope
so they could
cope.

But this disease?
It never leaves,
and names
don't change
a thing.

Matching Toenails to Heart

I'm at a salon—
No-Fail Nails—
which feels a little
bit
like jail
for your feet.

Some people
think of this
as a treat.
But to me,
a pedicure
is torture.
Boring!

I'd rather have
action
than relaxing.
I guess
you always wish
for what
you don't
already have.

"Do you enjoy?"
asks the older lady
who is scrubbing
my toes.

I shrug.
"It's a gift certificate.
From somebody
at Here's-A-Wish."

"Oh, how nice!"

Not really.
My feet aren't into
touchy-feely.

"Your name is Faith?"
asks the lady.

I nod. Make an effort
to smile.

"Faith Hope."
I've got to try harder
not to mope.
It's not her fault
that I'm sick.

"Pretty. It's a name
that reminds you.
You never forget
to have faith!"

Lame.
I've heard
too many jokes
about my name
to laugh.
I'm half-asleep
anyway.

The lady pats dry
one foot. She opens
the polish.

"The color is nice."

I picked "Blue Ice."
The color of my heart,
on the inside, as I
imagine it to be.

The lady paints.
She doesn't shake.
Her hands are steady.
My toes are ready
for anything.

I wish
my heart
could say
the same.

Wintertime

Outside,
inside,
all the time
wintertime.

Cold ice,
not nice,
tiny mice,
frozen slice:
wintertime.

No reason.
No rhyme.
Why's it got to be
mine:
wintertime?

Bummer.
I so
want summer.
Popsicles.
Not icicles.

This pedicure tickles
                                 my

                                              toes.

Main Street

No-Fail Nails
is on Main Street,
Seafoam,
right down the
road from my home.

There's snow,
but I walked
anyway.
That's what Uggs
are for.
     (That poor sheep
     who gave her wool
     to warm my feet.)

After the pedicure
I decide to turn right
and go to Pizza Delight
for a bite
to eat.

I'm beat.
Somebody in their teens
should not be
this sleepy!
(Or this weepy either.)

Can tears *freeze*?
I sneeze.

My breath
floats
before my face,
a hazy cloud
of the wintertime

inside
and
out.

Still on the Outside
While Inside Pizza Delight

Pizza Delight
smells
delish.
I wish
I could live
inside
this smell.

They should sell
this smell.

The bell dings
when I walk through
the door.

It's four
o'clock.
The place rocks
with kids
from Seafoam High.

I'm homeschooled.

I'm not cool.

Nobody knows
me unless they know
our funeral home.

Invisible. Dismal to be
me. Maybe I'm already
a ghost. Nobody knows
I am
here.

I order a slice.
Stare at neon lights.
Wish with all my might
that somebody
would just say "Hi."

Why
must
I
always
be
on
the
O U T S I D E?

My Noisy Joisey Uncle

St. Mark's
Lutheran Church
is always open,
and so I stop
on the way home.

It's warm inside.
And dim
wintertime light
shines
through the bright
stained glass
windows.

Candles flicker.
Nobody bickers.
Winter melts away
in this place,
and there's just
the quiet peace
of wooden seats:
empty pews
with hymnals
closed, not open.

Nobody sings.
This brings me
peace.

(I am the niece of
the choir director.
And not to judge,
but Uncle Hector
can be very
very
noisy.
He's from
"Joisey." His words,
not mine.)

I find
my place
and close
my eyes
to pray.

"Hey!" says a man's
voice. Oh boy.
Joy.
It's my noisy
Joisey uncle.
Great.

"Hey," I say.

"What's up, buttercup?
How's it shakin', bacon?
Having a great day, babycakes?"

"Sure," I say.
"It's always a great day
when I can stay
alive, right?"

"Right on, little fawn.
Cheers, pretty deer!"

I smile.
The best strategy
for dealing
with weird
Uncle Hector
is this:

Laugh at his random jokes.
Pretend his rhymes rock.
Don't watch the clock.

"So, what
are you doing here
on a Thursday afternoon,
silly goon?"

"I pop in
sometimes," I reply.
"Just to, like, pray.
Meditate.
Think about how great
it is
to be alive."

I try to smile.

"And I get all Zen,"
I add. "I just relax.
Breathe. Let it be."

What I don't tell
Uncle Hector
is that sometimes
I heckle
and nag
the man upstairs,
begging him again
and again
to just let me get
that brand-new heart.

So far,
God has taken lessons
from my mom.
He just ignores
me.

Outside the Church

There's a little bird,
wings weighted with snow.
It's stuck.
"I get it," I say
to the small creature.
"I can't fly either."

Tiny black eyes
look up
at me.
It chirps
in a help-me-please
kind of way.

"Don't worry," I say.
"I've got this."

I whisk snow
from its wings
with my glove.
It looks at me
with something
like love.

And then the
tiny bird lifts,
drifting high
into the sky,
wings spread
wide:

JUST ONE SMALL
BLACK DOT
AGAINST ALL
ETERNITY.

I can
relate.

The Sickest Baby

I burst
into this world
with
thin skin
the color
of pearls:
skeletal-white,
tinged with
blue.

The room
was the color
of mint,
Mom said.
A nice light
pastel green.

I was
the sickest baby
that midwife
had ever
seen.

By the Age of Three

I had an
entire team
studying me
and my disease
at CHOP:
Children's Hospital
of Philadelphia,
and then at
Johns Hopkins.

"It's tough," Mom said.

"So rough," Dad said.

I understood enough

about what
was happening.
I knew that my heart
was crappy.

A slacker of a ticker,
and not enough air
in my lungs
or in my blood.

I knew that
my life
was
crud.

Christmas Wish

Every year
for Christmas,
I'd ask Santa
for a new heart.

"Ho, ho, ho!"
Santa laughed.
"Isn't there a toy
or a game
that you
would like,
Faith?"

He knew my name,
but what Santa
obviously did not
know
was that
my heart
was
lame.

I Painted Hearts

I drew and doodled
        and used up
                all the crayons
                        and all the colors
just making hearts.

Big hearts,
        little hearts,
                the most perfect hearts
                    that a girl
                    could ever want.

So What Exactly Is Wrong

With you anyway?
Why
can't you play
like a normal
neighbor?
Do me a big favor
and fill me in,"
said red-headed
Eddy McGinn
when we were ten.

"I don't really like to
run," I said. "I just
get out of breath.
Now I have to go in.
The sun
is burning
my head."

I guess
I didn't
confess to
Eddy McGinn
that it was
predicted
I'd be dead
by the time
I was nineteen.

We Are the Stevens

Of Stevens Brothers
Funeral Home,
33 Main Street,
Seafoam, Delaware.

We are the Stevens
who fix the hair
of the deceased
and who care
to place
makeup
upon
pale faces
so they
look *great!* …

and not just …
late.

We are the Stevens
who deal
with the dead,

along with
the bereaved
and the bereft
and the broken-hearted
grief

of the families
of the deceased.

But for real,
we
can't seem
to deal

with me …
or with
my
disease.

No Matter What

I get home—which actually
is Stevens Brothers
Funeral Home. Dead
people downstairs,
live humans upstairs—
after plowing
through
the snow
with my shiny
new toes
inside my
boots.

I'm out of breath.
Out of energy.
I throw off my coat.
Pull off my Uggs.
Plop down
on the
old Victorian couch.
The grandfather clock
chimes, reminding me
that time
never stops.
It just clip-clops along,

like a stubborn old
horse.
Of course,
that's time for you,
all self-centered.
Whatever.

Victorian houses
often seem eerie:
Squeaks and creaks,
like the house speaks
to itself.
Our house
is sometimes too quiet.
And it feels haunted by
all the ghosts
we host.

It's quiet today.
"Hello," I say,
a test to
the rest
of my family.
"Anybody home?"

And then I can
hear that we have
a visitor:
Great-Aunt Mary.
Hector's mother.
My father's oldest sister
from a different mister.
        (My family tree is twisted.)

Just another Stevens
relative, my Great-Aunt
Mary.
But she's actually
my favorite
one of the bunch.

She's like the sun.

"All that matters
is love,"
says Great-Aunt Mary,
who is kind of like
an antique fairy.

She's old, but bold,
and she wears the most
amazing vintage
lace dresses

with
crazy tights
and bright-red
shiny go-go dancer
knee-high
boots.

Dad says she has a screw loose.
Mom says it was all that weed
she used to smoke back
in her 1960's hippie days.

But all I know
is that
Great-Aunt Mary,
the antique fairy,
really does care,

and that I dig
her big
frizzy hair,
which is
colored like a
sizzly rainbow.

"I know
you will be fine."
Mary smiles.
"It just might
take a while.

Be patient and
wait.
Fate will arrive.
Just be
alive. And remember,
Faith,

all that matters
is the love inside.

Even if your heart does
not work right …
There is always the love
inside."

Mom Is the Queen of Denial

"I should make
a will,"
I say to Mom
the next day.

She ignores me.
Just keeps filling
the sugar jar.

"This won't
go away,"
I say.

Mom closes her eyes,
as if she's going to pray.

"Faith," she says,
"You don't have anything
to leave behind
anyway.

When—*if*—
if-if-if!

you go, there will be
nothing left
on this earth
that's worth
a penny."

"Except Lenny," I say.
  (Lenny is my little brother.
  He's eight: a late-life
  Miracle Baby
  for Mom and Dad.)

"Plus there's my guitar.
And my car,
the old hearse.
Plus my purple
Dooney and Bourke
purse.

The bike I never ride.
The poetry I write.

The heart-shaped bracelet
you gave me
when I was eight.

My jewelry from Grandma …
My drawings …
I can go on and on."

Mom says nothing.
She just dumps
that sugar from the bag,
scattering sweet granules
all over the floor.

"We can't just ignore
this," I say.

"Are we making cookies?"
asks my brother,
running like a wild thing
into the kitchen.

His sneakers
squeak
on the linoleum floor.

Mom ignores
him too.

I hug my brother.
"Yep," I say. "Maybe.
Maybe chocolate chip."

"I want snickerdoodles!"
Lenny says. "Oodles and
oodles of snickerdoodles!"

"Me too!"

"Shhh," Mom says.
"This place sounds like
a zoo."

"It's not like we'll
wake the dead," I say.

Mom just walks
away.

She is the
queen
of denial.

She likes to defy
the idea
of me
not being
alive

while the queen
still breathes.

A Fail of the Heart

You don't want
to know
every detail.

It's basically
a fail
of the heart.

A congenital
defect
that will
affect
my life
      until
      the day
      I
      die.

The Other Hearts

In our household

are fine.

All hearts,

that is,

except for

mine.

Homework and Dead Bodies

"Faith, did you do your
homework?" asks Dad.

"All I have is math."

I'm crashed
on our saggy old
black sofa,
chilling with the
remote control,
channel-surfing.

Lenny is at school.
And Mom is swimming
her laps
at the rec center pool.

Dad is wearing
his dark-blue suit
with the white tie.
This means that
somebody has died.

> (One part of Dad's job
> is that he has to
> pick up
> the body
> and bring it back.
> It's wack, I know,
> but there you go.
> That's life, right?)

"Please get your homework
done *now*," Dad says.
"Stop slacking. Stop
procrastinating, Faith.
Never wait
for later."

His phone beeps and he
checks the text, looking
all perplexed, wrinkling
his forehead.

"What's next?" he says.
Dad shakes his head.

Obviously, somebody
else is dead.

Welcome to my life,
where dead people
rule the schedule.

Home + School = Homeschool

So
not cool.
No bull,
dude.

Homeschool
is
way full
of
rules
too,
just
like
real
school.

Home – School = the Same
Lame
Equation

Why I Am Homeschooled

It's because

of my health.

It's not because

of our wealth,

or anything to do

with the Bible Belt.

It's just because

I was dealt

a bad hand

by the man

upstairs.

You Don't See

A lot of other kids
when you
are homeschooled.
But don't be fooled.

You do get to see people.

Your family. Your preacher.
Your mom the teacher.
Your mom the teacher.
Blah,
             blah,
                          blah ...
Your
mom
the
teacher.

My mother
is like wintertime:
they both go
             on
                     and
                          on
                                   and
                                        on ...

49

Global Warming

Is making the weather
crazy.

One Monday in January,
there is

SO

much

snow …

There is nowhere
to
go.

It just blows and
blows.
The wind
cuts like cold
scissors.

It is
a frigging
blizzard!

                     I wish I were
             a wizard
        and could
    wave a wand
like magic.

I'd make my life
    not so tragic.
        And I'd make the
           weather actually
              act normal.

When the Snow Stops

I decide to go
outside. I want to
try to sled with Lenny.

We fly down the hill
behind our house.
And my brother
is just
loving it.

"Okay," I say.
"Time to go in."

Lenny has a little
conniption fit.

"No way!"

"Yes way!"

"Why?"

I try
to explain.

"I can't make
it back up the hill
another time.
It makes me too
tired."

"Geez beez, Faith.
You are like an old
lady."

His cheeks are red.
Lenny shakes his head.

"Time to go to bed!" Lenny says
in a sing-song voice.
"Old lady Faith has no choice."

"If I could climb that hill,
I would rejoice," I reply.

"Just try.
Please. Pretty please
with a cherry on top?"

A cop stops.
"You two okay?" he calls
from his car.

"I'm fine!" Lenny yells.

I'm not.

And the truth is:
I'm
really
not
okay
with
that.

I'm Always Cold

Mom takes me to
the coffee shop.
This is my favorite place
in town.

We sit down.
Order lattes.
Gingerbread
with cinnamon.

I sip the warm
liquid.
So good.
So hot.
Everything I am
not.

"So the caffeine isn't great
for your heart, Faith,"
Mom says.
"But every now
and then
it's okay
in moderation."

Drinking this coffee
is
like a *vacation*,
in the coffee
shop
with
Mom.

"Everybody
needs
a
treat
every
now
and
then,"
Mom says.

.

"Just enjoy," she says.
"Carpe diem! Seize
the day!"

"Okay," I say.
I take another sip.

Mom lifts her cup.
Clinks it to mine.

"Cheers!"

> She will never
> talk
> about
> our
> fears.

It's Been a Long Winter

Springtime is finally here—
finally!—
and so Mom takes me to *Sears*.
>   (Not Gap. Not Pac-Sun. Not the Deb Shop
>   or Body Central or Wet Seal or What's Your Deal.
>   Sears! Oh. Dear.)

"May is a fine time
for new clothes,"
Mom says. "A super-duper
new wardrobe
for my gorgeous
girl!"

(Neither
of us
points
out
the
fact
that
I have
lost
way
too
much
weight
lately.

I used
to be
a size
2.

Now
I am
just
a 0.

A
big
fat
0.)

I watch a girl—
a *normal* girl—
who must be a size
10. She is my hero.
I wonder when—*if!*—
I will ever fit into
a 10.

Mom holds up
a strange orange
conservative shirt
and a random pair
of capri geek pants
that a middle-aged
underweight lady
would wear.

"I swear," I say,
turning away.
"You wouldn't
catch me dead
in that outfit."

Mom bites her lip.

I slip through
the Juniors
section, where glittery
gowns shout out
that the prom
will soon come.
The dumb
old prom.

"Let's go, Mom."
I'm fighting tears
right here in Sears.

Crying in public
is one of my worst
fears.

When you're the
daughter of an
undertaker,
you learn to be
a pretty good
faker.

Hippie Girl

I'm an old soul
in a young body
that doesn't work
quite right.

Kind of
a 1960's hippie girl
giving it a
psychedelic whirl
in a twenty-first
century world.

Maybe I take
after
Great-Aunt Mary.

I like
my bell-bottoms
wide,
embroidered with
butterflies,
and my T-shirts
tie-dyed.

Daisy chains
in long straight hair.
And nobody cares
if I bare
my
belly button.

(I'm skinny,
and it is
an innie.)

And anyway,
that navel
is just
living proof
of the fact
that Mom and me
were once
attached.

Nobody Sings Along

On the way home
from the mall,
I don't feel like
talking.
Neither does Mom
for once in her
lifetime.
I'm driving
and
we're quiet.
And there's only
the songs on the radio—
songs we both know—
but nobody
sings
along.

"Stay strong," Mom says
when I pull into
the circle of our driveway.
"Keep the faith, Faith."

Surprise

When we go inside,
Dad has a surprise.
"Guess what?"

I shrug.

"We're going away
next week.
Somewhere fun.
Somewhere sunny."

I shrug again.

"I'll give you a hint:
Orlando! Bam! Shazam!"

"*Disney?!*"
Lenny freaks.
"Next week?
Sweet!"

I just smile.
Sometimes it takes
me a while
to react
to good news
like that.

I'm on this list—

a waiting list for a brand-new
heart—
and so we're part
of this
Here's-A-Wish
thing
in which
they assist
in making
wishes
come true.

What I really wish
is that my hair
was blue.

Or that it wasn't true
that I completely need
a new
heart.
>(I need to get
>that ticker
>quick.
>Before I kick
>the bucket.)

What I really wish
is that I drove a car
that wasn't the
ex-hearse for our
family business.

But a major part
of the Here's-A-Wish
Foundation
is that they want you
to have a great
vacation
before you die.
And that is
why
they pay
to fly
you
to Disney.

In the Airplane

Floating high
in the blue June sky,

cutting through
mounds of *marshmallow
clouds*,
I wonder why

people assume
that the afterlife

is sky-high.

"Why does heaven
have to be

over our heads,
so out of reach

until we
are dead?"
I ask.

But Mom is snoring
beside me.

I know
it's not over

till the fat lady sings,
but what if

we got our wings
while we were
still alive?

What if
we can't drive
in this so-called
afterlife?

What if
we have to fly
there
in an airplane?

All this thinking
is hurting my brain.

Flying
is
a
pain.

Peer Pressure in Heaven

But what
if I
don't want
to be
an angel?

Can
something
different
be arranged?

I don't want all the
other
angels to
think
I am strange.

The Airplane Lands

And my entire
family is way
too excited.
Hyper.
People stare.
And my parents don't
even care.
This is what happens
when you get
out of Delaware.

"Whoopee!" screams Mom.
"Whoo-hoo!" bellows Dad.
"We're here!" yells Lenny.
"Yippee!"

They high-five.
They fist-bump.
They **jump**.

They mortify me.

I'm too beat
to scream.
Too tired
to be all fired
up.

"Shut up," I mutter.

It's such a bummer
to be sick,
and even
the dead
Mr. Disney
can't fix
some things.

Castles and Magic

Nighttime.

The first
sparkly bursts
of fireworks
are shooting,
zooming high.

Fireworks explode,
sizzle
fizzling patterns in
the tattered black
summertime sky.

"I really like this place!"
Lenny's face
is so full of joy.

I really love that boy.

I lean my head
on Dad's shoulder.

"I'm just wishing
that I
could be
a princess
in frothy pink,
working at Disney,
just wishing
for the end
of my shift,
rather than being
me.
I wish
I wasn't
on this list.
I wish
I wasn't
sick."

Dad just listens.
His eyes glisten.

When
you
wish
upon
a
star,
it
never
gets
you
very
far.

Eating Lunch

In the sunshine
the next day,
I have a hunch
that my mom
and my dad
are crying inside,

trying not to fight
about my right
to live my life
with a heart
that's totally mine:

One that does no wrong.
One
that doesn't belong
to somebody else.

"I wish I could be
Mickey Mouse!" says Lenny,
bouncing in his
seat.

"Who do you wish to be,
Faith?"

"Um, I wish I were
an elf.
I wish I liked
being myself.
I wish
I could just sit
on a shelf,
hidden,
and only
come out
at
Christmas."

Lenny just looks
at me. Mom and Dad
look away.

And then Lenny
asks if we all
want to pray.

A Bob Marley Song

Is playing,
and he's saying,
"One love!
One heart!"
This song fits
like a glove,
lighting up
our lunch,
and I
suddenly can't
get enough
of it.

I keep the beat,
dance in my seat,
tap my feet,
continue to eat.

But then
I remember
Bob Marley
is gone,
and this is just
some dumb
song.

It
all
feels
so
wrong.

Did You Ever Notice

How many songs
include hearts?

"Total Eclipse
of the Heart" and
"Take Another Piece
of My Heart" and
"Stop Draggin'
My Heart Around" and
"Don't Go Breaking
My Heart."

There's "Heartbreak Hotel"
And "Sgt. Pepper's
Lonely Hearts Club Band"
and "Heart of a Man."

There's "Heart of
Stone" and
"Heart of
Gold" and
"My Heart Has a Mind of Its Own."

The ring tone
on my phone
is "Headed for a
Heartbreak,"
from 1988.

When my phone
rings,
I am reminded
every single time
of my fate
just before I say
"Hello."

Bucket List

Maybe I'll get dreads
before I'm dead.
Or a small red dot
in the center
of my forehead:
a third **eye**
before I die.
Or a tiny
diamond chip
to shimmer
on the side
of my nose.
Maybe I'll
tattoo a
yellow rose
on each
of my
toes.
Or learn
to sew.
Yeah … no.

I'll belt out
"I Will Survive"
while I'm
still alive.
And I won't even care
if people
roll their eyes.

I'll bake lots of pies.
Plan a surprise party
for Grandma …
Shazam!

I'll make homemade jam.
I'll play in a band.
Spend time with my fam.

I'll go on trips—
hipster trips—
and paint my lips
for my bucket list.

Sleep alone beneath
the Northern Lights
in an igloo dome
in Iceland.
Go to Rome.
Get out of Seafoam.

I'll bathe a baby elephant
in Thailand.
Give a miniature
giraffe a bubble bath.

Maybe I'll go to the prom
without even having to ask Mom.
I'll wear a shimmery gown
and a corsage on my wrist
and make braids
with French twists,
all because of my
bucket list.

Maybe I'll climb mountains
and dance through fountains
in places not allowed,
because who is going
to arrest
a girl who will soon
be dead?

I'll climb
the Eiffel
Tower, eat
wildflowers,
find my
superstar girl powers
before I leave
this world.

I'll dive for
           pearls, learn
                   to swim,
           skydive on a
                   whim,
                       maybe even fall
                       in love …
                       with *him*.

Do pirouettes
on the rim
of the Grand Canyon,
wearing a pink tutu
and ballet shoes.

Sit in the front row
of a rock concert
by U2.

Maybe I'll
get a companion
animal—a dog with
pink paws—
from the rescue place.

And I'll even say grace.
Wear purple lace.

Press my face
to the glass
before I pass.

Seeing everything.
Breathing everything.
Believing everything.
Eating everything.
Hearing and feeling
everything I never wanted
to miss …
All the everythings
on my

bucket list.

In the Disney Hotel

I tell Lenny about
my bucket list
because he's
too young
to get all shocked.

"That rocks," he says
when I finish.
"I love you, sissy."
His brown eyes look misty.

I love the sprinkle of freckles
smattering his nose
and his cowlicks
and his small chubby toes.

I love how he knows
about my disease,
but he doesn't make
that everything about me.

"If you could wish for any
kind of heart in the whole wide
world, what kind of heart would
you like?" Lenny asks.

"One like yours," I reply.

"One like mine?" Lenny asks,
and I nod my head in the night.

"One that works just right.
One that's full of light."

A Heart Like Ringo Starr

I want a heart
that keeps
the beat
of me
perfectly,
in dreamy
seamless
rhythm:

Never missing.

Never skipping.

Never dropping

the sticks.

I want a heart
that ticks.
That tocks.
A cardio clock
that rocks.
That knocks to
the beat
of me.

I want a heart
like a
dead-on
drummer,
never a bummer,
like the backbeat
of a **Beatles**
summer.

I want a heart
like a drummer,
a heart
like Ringo Starr,
a heart
to take me
far.

Boyfriend

Lenny is obsessed
with the idea
of me getting
a boyfriend
before it's
the end.
Before it's
too late.
Before fate
takes me away,
an old maid
like in his
favorite
card game.

"You need to find
your knight
in shining armor,"
Lenny says.

"Maybe he'll ride
right into your life
on a big white horse.
He'll carry a sword.
Or maybe he'll be a prince
at a dance,
taking some big chance
to fit a shoe
on your big ugly foot,
like in 'Cinderella.'
Or maybe he'll be like
Spiderman, some cool
superhero who can
save your life!"

"Yeah, right," I say.

"Or maybe he'll look
like Shrek, but be a heck
of a nice guy."

I sigh.

"Life isn't like
a fairy tale, Len.
When it all ends,
there's not really
a happily
ever after."

Lenny ignores me.
He must be taking lessons
from Mom.

"I want your husband
to be like Ben," he says.
      (Ben is his best friend.)

"Ben is eight. Too young to
date," I say.

"I just mean that I want your
guy to be nice, like Ben.
Cool like him. I want him to
be awesome, like somebody
who can save the world.
A guy who can fly!
Somebody I like, who can
actually save your life."

"Peter Pan can fly."

"He's not your kind
of guy," Lenny says.
"We need somebody
with the power
to keep you alive."

Lenny totally doesn't get
the concept of death …
or the idea
of boyfriends
either.

"I think I have a
fever," I say.
"Let's call it a day."

"Sweet dreams, sissy,"
Lenny says,
and he gets up
from his bed,
comes over,
and like always,
kisses
the top
of my head.

I'll miss that
when I'm dead.

Our Song

Lenny and I have this
evening routine.

We sing our favorite
Beatles song—
"Hey Jude"—
as our lullaby
each night.

What Lenny
doesn't know,
though,
is that
I sometimes
change the words
in my mind.

Hey dude

Don't
be
afraid
of
this
girl
named
Faith.
Take
a
sad
song
and
make
it
better.
Remember to let her
get better …
wherever, whoever
you are.
Remember to let her
under your skin …
then you begin

to make her better.

The Lullabies

That soothed me
the most
were the songs
of the Rolling Stones,

Pink Floyd,

Led Zeppelin,

the Grateful Dead …
        (I was a rather
        strange baby.)

the notes
roll on
in
my head.

Classic, not spastic.
No plastic bands.
No elastic pants.

Vinyl, eight-tracks,
cassettes …
That's the music
that's in my head
and will be
until I'm
dead.

If I Ever Find a Guy

Who likes
old rock and roll,
my whole soul
will know.

If I ever find a guy
who likes
classic rock,

my heart will

ticktock-

ticktock-

ticktock …

After the Magic Kingdom

We drive south
to the beach
in our small green
Spark rental car.
It is the last day
of the trip,
and Lenny is flipping
out.

"I don't want to go
home! Can we just
stay one more day?
Please? Please?"

"Stop whining.
You are driving me
crazy," I say.
"There's an end to
everything."

Waves crash
around our feet:
my entire family
ankle-deep
in the Atlantic Ocean.

I pick up a broken
shell, and I write
"*Goodbye*"
in the sand.

"I hate to say
goodbye too," I say
to my brother.
"Maybe in my other
life I was a mermaid."

I always hate
to leave the sea.

Maybe I'll hate
to leave this earth too.

But there's not too
much I can
do
about
it
now.

We are people.
We leave.
But that means
we go
somewhere
new
and maybe better
than
where we are now.

Getting Back to the Family Business

After being at Disney
makes me dizzy.

Death is so
busy.

People just keep
dying, defying life.

Funerals are big
business.

The Stuff of Being a Stevens

Caskets, weeping
basket cases,
faces strained
with pain.

Cremation
is no vacation,
even though

ashes are
in fashion.

A celebration!
Focus on the good times,
the things that made
you smile.
You had her
for a nice long while.

Tissues, issues.
Bless you.

Funeral bouquets,
a haze and daze.

I'll pray for you.
Rest in peace.
So sad about your niece.
What else did he want to do?
Your grandpa was in World War II?
He was a good man.
She lived a nice life.
I'm sorry about
your wife.
Your sister got such a bad deal.
Is everyone staying for the
meal?

I Have a Confession

Those funeral processions?
When the lines of cars all
follow one another to the
cemetery, headlights on,
little white magnetic
flapping flags,
hearse in the back.

Sometimes I slack
and crack my gum,
jamming along
to some
good song
on the radio,
you know?

I go
a little too slow,
and I just know
that I'm nothing
but
happy
to be alive
as I open the windows
and drive.

The Amazing Heart!

Step right up!
Learn about your
heart: the incredibly
amazing organ!

Did you know
that your heart
keeps beating
even
when separated
from the rest
of your body?
It has its own
special
electrical
impulse.

That
is awesome-sauce.

It beats
two and a half billion times
in your lifetime.

Center of your chest,
a little to the left,
some hearts work best.
Others, like mine,
are a hot mess.

It's the size of a fist.
Sometimes when I'm
pissed,
I wish
I could just punch
the one
who made
me
this way.

Heart Box

I saved a heart-shaped,
lace-draped
box from Valentine's Day
a few years ago.
This was from
before my
heart fail
was known
by the general
public.

The red box
still smells sweet,
like minty-cream candy,
like melted sugar,
like delicious chocolate
long gone.

The red box
is just right
for the small things
I want to keep,
like the poems
and songs
I write.

It bites
that my heart
doesn't work
right.

That's why
I write.

The red box
is full of words:
slips of pink paper
scribbled with pencil
slivers of my heart,
slices of my whole
soul ...
poems written
by a girl
who will never
grow old.

Different Lists

"Maybe there are just
a whole bunch
of different lists,
written by the man
upstairs," I say to
Great-Aunt Mary one day.

"One of the lists—
my list—
            (which makes me
            way pissed)
is people with
heart fails.
Another one
is people who
will be killed
in car crashes.
Another one
is random people
who
never get to
live their passions.

There is the You-Will-
Be-Murdered-By-A-Wacko
list.

The You-Will-
Go-From-Smoking-Tobacco
list.

Another one
is for those who
end up with cancer.

And the last list
is for people who
just pass away
gently
from old age."

Great-Aunt Mary shrugs.
She grins.

"This world is just
a stage
for people living
different lists,"
she says.

"I know, right?" I reply.
"Nobody gets off
the planet
alive.
We all will die.

All I want to know
is …
why?"

Guidelines for Heart Transplants

There are more than
84,000 of us
here in the
U.S.
on the
organ
transplant
list.

It's more like a pool
than a list, though.

What most people
don't know
is that
there's a lot
to consider:
tissue, blood type,
size.

Even where you
live.

Whoever gives
me a heart
will most likely
live in a place
that's close
to mine.

The gift of
a lifetime.

Somebody else
will have to die

to keep me

alive.

Part 2:

OFF THE HOOK

It's Early in the Morning

And I can hear
Dad on the phone,

even though his
voice is low.

"Really? Seriously?

Vinnie Green?
Oh, that is so
sad. Too bad."
Dad hangs up.

"What?" I ask.

There Was a Crash

Just down the road
from our place
late last night
while we slept.

A driver lost
control. A car flipped
                   and rolled
                   over and over.
It ended up
in the creek,

in Black Creek.

It was a boy
who lived down
the street.

It was Vinnie Green.
He was the same age
as me.

Vinnie Green's body
was found, drowned,
in Black Creek.

Vinnie Green's heart
was probably
strong, and this is so
totally
wrong.

Life is not a
song.
Life is not
a fairy tale.

I wish I could bail.
Vinnie Green's end
was *so* not fair …

And I wonder
where
he
is
now.

Dad's Phone Rings Again

And this time,
his voice gets high.
"Oh my!" he says.
"That would be sublime."

His cheeks flush.
I've never seen my
dad blush.
He hangs up in a rush.

"Faith," he says,
all breathless.
"Pack a bag.
We need to get
to Johns Hopkins
as *fast* as we can
for a transplant.
They have a heart
for you!"

Is this true?
I have no clue.

"You will be brand new," says Dad
I am frozen to one spot,
shocked.

"Hurry!" Mom shouts.

"But ... but ...
Wait! What?!
Doesn't Lenny have to go
to school?"

"Aunt Mary is staying," Mom replies.
She flies around the house
getting ready.

I feel
unsteady.

My head is
too full.

This will be so cool ...

if it's really
true.

Highway Blur

The highway is a blur.

My eyes   feel like fur.

Dad drives like crazy.

My mind   is hazy.

Driving the Heart

"Do you know that
the heart has a driver?" Dad says.
"Like a guy who drives the heart
as fast as he can, packed in ice,
to get it to the hospital in time."

My eyes are wide.

Driving the heart?

Dad has Mozart playing.
I'm kind of praying.
Mom keeps saying,
over and over,
"I can hardly believe
this is really true.
It feels so surreal."

How do they think
I must
feel?

Is this really real?

The Hospital

Is a worse blur
than the road trip.
Mom's face is white.

"Are you all right?" I ask.
But she does not
answer.

Dad is flipping out,
spazzing,

his face frazzled.
"Hurry!" he yells at a nurse.
He is too full of worry.
Everything
is
blurry.

White Gown

Opens in the back.
This is wack.
Nobody wants to see

a

crack.

I kind of wish
to just go back
home
and make do,
get along
with my old
familiar
heart.

It wasn't all that bad.

Was it?

IV

Line.
Fine.

Don't
whine.

Don't
cry.

I
am
high,
sky-high.

Eyes
shine
down
on
me.

Green
masks
on
faces.

Amazing
grace.

I
won't
cry.

I
won't.
float.

Twilight Sleep

Somebody

Says

1
2
3

Deep

1
2
3

Beep
Beep

3

Deep

Deep

Sleep

It Takes Work

To get awake.
I take a while.

A
long
time.

My eyes
won't open.
I am hoping
for something …

                    But …
                    what?

Then I remember.
This is not
a dream.

Mom's here,
sitting near
the bed.

Dad beams
down at me,
like God.

The Father.
"Honey," he says.
"You have a brand-new heart.
This is a brand-new start."

I just
fart.

How Does It Feel?

Does it feel real?

                                     Am I ready for a meal?

It'll take a while to heal.

                                     I spin like a wheel.

What's the deal?

                                     Is this really real?

How does it really feel …

                                     anyway?

Give me just another

                                     day,

and then maybe

                                     I can say.

Days into Weeks

I'm kind of a geek.
Weak.
Not really speaking
much.
Out of
touch.

New hearts
aren't easy
to adjust.

Bionic

"I wonder
whose heart
you got?" says Lenny.
"You're kind of
a robot now,
with some dead
girl's heart.
Like, bionic.
Supersonic."
Ironic.
I don't feel
bionic.
I just feel …
moronic.

Having a new heart
isn't as wicked cool
as I'd imagined.
Getting a transplant
isn't all it's cracked up
to be.

Rain, Pain, Can't Explain

"You should be ecstatic!" Mom says.
"You are blessed!" Pastor Dan says.
"So lucky!" Dad adds.
"Bionic Faith!" Lenny raves.

I really do need
to behave.
"I'm sorry for being
such a grump.
I've been a grouch."

Ouch.
Even sitting on the couch
sends little knives of pain
flying through me
like sharp rain.
Sharp heart rain.
It's hard to explain.

It is raining on the
inside of me,
and that's a sucky
way to be.

Yes, I am lucky.
Yes, I'm blessed.
I should be ecstatic.

But I'm not.
This rain and
this pain
and this can't explain
are all I've got.

My happiness
is shot.

Rejection

"Your body
may be rejecting
the new organ,"
says Dr. Morgan.

"Most transplants
experience about two
rejection episodes.
Don't worry.
It's fairly normal.
But
it's not for sure.
We need
to give it
a bit
more time."

I feel
like slime.
Pond slime.
Pond scum.
Bummer.
What a way
to end my
summer.

Just a Few Weeks Later

It's all good.
My body has
stopped attacking
itself. My immune
system has chilled
out.

Rejection

episodes

are

over.

Seafoam High

They say
that I can go
to the public
school,

SEAFOAM HIGH,

if I want.

"Fine," I reply.
This is a lie.
Nothing is
fine.

I'm walking around
with a heart
that's not even
mine.

"Prom," says Mom.
"It'll be the bomb," says Lenny.

"Senior trip," says Dad.
"You already dress so hip," says Mom.

"Maybe a boy will kiss
you," says Lenny.
"You will get a boyfriend!"

I leave the room.
Boom. Doom.
I am not looking forward to
school.
I am not cool.
I will never get a
boyfriend.

The.
End.

First Day

I have to pray.
      I don't know what
            to say.

Being a senior

      at Seafoam High
is no pie in the sky.

I am an outsider.
      People stare.
            Don't care.

I am a freak.

How will I ever
        get
            through
                this week?

I Am the Girl

With a random
dead person's heart
keeping me alive.
Somebody else
had to die
so that I
could be alive.

This is not right.

These halls
are
way
too bright.

This light
hurts
my eyes.

I am blind.

Maybe I am
not
thankful to be
alive.

Maybe I should
find
my donor.

Why do I
even try?

I am a loner.
I am the girl
who breathes—
Who eats! Who sleeps!
Whose heart beats!—
because of an organ
donor.

I am the biggest loner
in Seafoam, Delaware.

I
Just
Don't
Care
Anymore.

I am such a bore.

They can all
just
ignore
me

Being a Ghost Before You're Dead

Science class,
and Ms. Gast
is talking about
how
certain things
don't mix.

Like oil and water.
"They are immiscible,"
she says.

I AM IMMISCIBLE.

I don't mix
with the kids
in this
school.

I am invisible
too.

And being a ghost
before you're dead
is *so*
not
cool.

In phys ed
I am dead.

I can't run.
I can't jump.
I can't bump
a volleyball
off the top
of my head.

I am dead.

I am excused
from physical
exertion.
I am not expected
to be connected
to anything regarding
cardiovascular
or massive muscular
endeavors.

Will I be like this
forever?

Awkward Is an Understatement

Everybody knows
I've had a heart
replacement.

I'm like a basement.
I'm the place
where nobody
wants to go.

The place that's full
of must and mold.

It's obvious by the
way they can't seem
to look me in the eye.

They just kind of look
to the side, as if
something has died
right in front
of them
and they can't
stand the
stench.

Awkward
is an understatement
when it
comes to
being me.

Freak of the Week

I actually wish
I could go back
in time to when
my heart was still
mine. I was kind of
fine, right?—
being homeschooled
and on the list.

At least there were
people who knew
I existed.

At lunch I sit
at a table with
all the misfits.

Freaks and geeks.
And I—Faith Hope Stevens—am
the
Freak of the Week.

The Freak of the Month.

The Freak of the Year.

I, Faith Hope Stevens,
am the Freak of All
Eternity.

Gossip

Some kid whispers,
"She doesn't look sick."

I CAN HEAR YOU!
That's what I want
to yell.

I'm sick as hell.
Maybe I look well,
but you don't live
on the inside of me.

It's so weird to be
the subject of gossip
and whispers
and rumors.

It's not cool to
be the one
big tumor
on the healthy body
of this school.

It

Is

So

Not

Cool.

Facebook

You know how
you can see some
people's Facebook posts,
even when
they are not
your friend?
Well, I was stalking
some of the kids in
my class, and I saw
a post by this guy
Dylan T. Horst.

"Sick chick
in my homeroom," he
posted. "Trying hard
not to stare."

I don't care.

My

life

is *so*

not

fair.

Twitter Is for Twits

Even freaks can tweet.
And so I do.

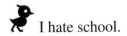 I hate school.

Nobody re-tweets.
Nobody favorites me.

Even in the Twitterverse,
I am the girl
who is
cursed.

Maybe I'll Be Happy in a Little While

Great-Aunt Mary
comes to see me.
She's all beamy,
like the moon,
like stars,
like cars on dark
nights.
Great-Aunt Mary
is full of light.

"Are you feeling all right?"
she asks.

"Do you want to dance?

Do you want to go and grab a bite
to eat?

Do you want me to rub
your feet?

How about we get
a pedicure?

Or go shopping?

Go for a nice walk
on the beach?

Collect seashells?

Eat peaches?

What will make you smile,
Faith?"

I think for a while.
"I don't know."

I really don't.

"How about we go
to Rehoboth and
look for sea glass?"

I shrug.

"Oh, don't be such a grump!

You're such a downer,"
Mary says.

She's trying to make me laugh,
clowning around.

I try
a half-smile.

"Maybe I'll get happy
in a little while," I say.

"Okay. Let's go. Let's go
to Rehoboth."

Dad Lets Me Take His Car

I drive, which is fine
with Mary.
Fairies don't like to drive.
They like to fly.

"So good for you
to get out of Seafoam!
Get out of that dark
old funeral home.
It'll be good for you
to just roam the beach.
Pick up sea glass,
just like when
you were a little girl.
First one to find purple
is a princess. You win!"

Great-Aunt Mary is always
like this.
She's so full of fizz.
Mary is like ginger ale:
good for what
ails
you.

I am already
feeling
better.

September in Rehoboth

Is the best.
It's not a crowded mess.

It's not so hot.
We find a parking spot.
I don't smell pot.
No spring break.

I don't have to fake
a smile.

I'll file this day
away
in my heart …

My brand-new heart …

And remember September
on the beach with my
Great-Aunt
Mary.

Searching for Sea Glass

I don't get
short of breath
or feel like death
as we walk and walk and walk
across wet sand,
barefoot,
looking for sea glass.

It feels so good.
Sand, water, waves.
Crashing, rolling,

          in,   out,
            in,   *out.*

I love this sound.

I take a big breath.
My heart is working fine.
I am alive!

I keep my eyes to the sand,
Searching for purple.
Searching for glass.
Searching for anything
that shines.

I Am the Winner

A guy
walking in the other
direction almost bumps
into me.

"Sorry!" he says.

I look up.
His eyes shine
squinty-dark.
His floppy straight hair
covers one
eye, and there's
a scar
shaped like a star
on his arm.
On his chest
is a tattooed
cross and a blue
word:

Believe

Hypnotized.
Mesmerized.
So surprised.
I can't stop
my stare.

His hair
blows in the
sea breeze.
Geez.
This guy is like my age,
but movie-star hot.
And shy he is not.

"What's your name?" he asks.
"Do you go to Mulane?"

"No, I go to Seafoam."

"Oh."

"My name is Faith. Faith Stevens.
I'm a senior. A senior at
Seafoam."

"Jimmy," he says.
His eyes glimmer.
He shimmers.
"Jimmy Winters,
and I live here.
I'm a senior too.
A senior at Mulane."

Now I know his name.
This is the best day ever.
He is a magnet,
attracting my energy
to his.

I suddenly remember
that Mary is here too.
"This is my aunt," I say.
"Mary."

He shakes her hand.
"Lovely to meet you,"
he says.

"I love your manners,"
says Great-Aunt Mary.

I can't believe my luck.
Today *so* does not suck.

And all of a sudden
right at my feet,
as water rushes,
there is a big chunk.
A hunk
of sea glass.
Purple. Of course.
I am the winner.

I have won
the sun.
I am the winner.
The biggest gift
of all
is meeting
this
Jimmy Winters.

Falling, Floating, Leaping

"Do you want to, like,
go for ice cream? Or something?"
he asks after Mary and I watch
him swim, strong arms stroking
across the rising high waves.

He is such a babe, dripping
drops of the sea
beside me. He smells like
sunshine and salt and lotion:
a magical ocean potion.

I look at Mary. She smiles.
"Go for ice cream,
darlin'," she says.
"I'll be sitting on that bench.
I have
a book in my purse,
of course,
plus my knitting.
I'll keep busy."

Mary points
to a boardwalk bench.
Jimmy Winters
shakes water
from his hair.
A few drops
land on my hand.

If not for the sand
beneath my feet,
I'd fall easily
to another
land.

I am falling,

falling,

falling

inside.

Ice Cream

So we go
to this place
called In Your Face,
which claims to have
more than four hundred
flavors. You can watch the waves
from pink and green tables
outside.

I order mint chocolate chip
in a cup, and Jimmy Winters
gets a chocolate cone
with sprinkles.

A few of the sprinkles
and a dot of chocolate
end up on his nose.

"You have some on your
face," I say. "On your nose."

"I know."
He laughs and dabs his face
with a napkin.
There's a sprinkle
on his lips.
And I wish
I could kiss
it off.
Then I start to cough.

I cough and cough,
like a fuzzy cloth
of love-crush or
something
is stuck in my
throat.

A boat
floats by,
way out
on the horizon,
and a silvery dolphin
leaps happy and free.

I know just how
that dolphin feels.
I know that boat:
how it is to float.

The moat
has been opened
to me.
I have the keys
to the castle.
I am the queen.
No longer the geek.

"Do you need CPR?
Are you okay?"

"I am totally okay," I say.
"As a matter of fact,
I am great."

Wait, is this
a date?
I don't hate
fate
anymore.

We Talk

And talk, and our insides are
melting into puddles, muddling
together
in the center
of that pink and green table.

Jimmy Winters tells me how he
was named for a famous actor—
James Dean—whose movies
he's never even seen.
And I tell about my name.
About the faith
and the hope
and the need to cope
for all these years.

I tell him about
Here's-A-Wish
and my bucket list
and going to Disney,
and how they didn't think
I'd live this long.
I tell him about
my heart transplant

and about how
there's a slight chance
for another rejection
episode.

I tell him about how
I used to be homeschooled
but not anymore.
Not this year,
and about how
that freaks me out.
I tell him about how
the kids
whisper
and stare.

"I love your hair,"
he says when I finish.
"It's cool
how it's blowing
like a curtain
across your face.
I love the way
you
smile too."

I know that I blush.
This is definitely a crush.

"And," says Jimmy Winters,
"you must have gotten an awesome
heart because I can see it shining out
through your eyes."

I sigh. This moment is so
groovy,
better than any romantic
movie
I've ever seen.
His eyes are lakes,
deep, deep lakes,
bottomless lakes,
with quicksand.
And I am drowning.

He has this chip
on his front tooth.
And it's so darn cute.

"So," I say.
"Let's talk about you."

Jimmy Winters tells me
how he loves to swim,
and how he came here today
on a whim.

He tells me how he gets straight As
in English and history.
But it's a mystery
as to why he fails
math.

He tells me about a cool path
behind his house
that leads through the woods
to an abandoned old foundation
of a basement,
where he and his band,
Family Spam,
like to jam.
   ("Hey!" I say.
   "I play too!")

He tells me about his family.
And about how his dad
served in the Middle East.
And how at least
he came home
alive.

He talks about
his cousin who
was his best friend.
And how that all
came to an end
a few months ago
when the cousin
was killed
in a wreck.
He tells me how
the car landed
in Black Creek—
actually near me!—
over in Seafoam.

"Wait!" I say.
"You mean
Vinnie Green?"

This is *way* weird.
Jimmy Winters's eyes are filled with tears.
I tell him how my family owns a funeral home and that we
did Vinnie Green's service.

"Wow. Just … wow," Jimmy says.

"How did it happen that we'd meet?" I say.
"It was meant to be," he says.
"Sent from heaven."
Wow. Just. Wow.

Jimmy tells me all about Vinnie Green:
How he loved refried beans
and Mexican food.
And how that dude
had the best heart
and cared so much about others

and had so much
love.

"And Vinnie
was an organ donor,"
says Jimmy Winters.
"So somebody else
is living
with his kidneys
and his liver
and his …
heart."

At the word "heart,"
we both
give a little start.
His eyes are wide.
I feel like I could cry.

"Holy Moses," Jimmy says.
"Holy crap. Do you think it's
possible …"

I shrug. I'm trembling,
shaking. The earth is
quaking inside
of me.

"Do you know
whose heart
you got?"

I shake my head.
"No. I didn't go there.
Not yet."

"Do you want to
find out?"

"Yeah. I kind of do.
Especially now."

Ripping

It's hard
to say goodbye
to this guy.
It's like I'm
being ripped
inside.

"Later," says Jimmy.
"We will chill."

"You have my number.
Hit me up."

"Definitely."

I am bereft
when we separate.
It's as if my soul
and Jimmy Winters's soul
were joined
with Velcro.

Leaving the beach,
leaving Rehoboth,
heading home,
I am
RIPPPPPING.

But then
my phone rings.

It's Him

"Hey," I say.

"Hey," he says.

"What's up?"
I try to sound casual,
like whatever,
but my voice is as wispy
as a feather.

"Are you home yet?"

"Almost," I say.
Great-Aunt Mary is
making motions at me
that mean
        HANG UP THE PHONE
        WHILE
        YOU
        ARE
        DRIVING.

"Can I come and get you?
Like tonight?
Maybe go for a hike?
Then get a bite to eat
for dinner?"

Jimmy Winters
wants to come
and get me!
He's taking me
out to eat!

I am happy
from head to feet.

"Sweet," I say.

"Like maybe
five o'clock?"

"That rocks."

"Oh, and text me
your address
for my nav."

"Yes! I will.
See you at five."

We say goodbye.
Mary winks.

I have never felt
so
alive.

I tell Mary about the date.

We celebrate.
She's cool like that.
We high-five.

"So what should I wear?" I ask.
"What's appropriate?
It's like a hike, plus dinner.
I wonder what Jimmy Winters
Will wear?"

"Probably pants," says Great-Aunt Mary.
And we both
crack up.

"Hope so."

I pull the car
into our driveway.

I
am
home.

Home

So I tell Mom and Dad all about it,
and they are happy.
Lenny is **bouncing** off the walls.

"Faithie has a boyfriend," he says
again and again.

"He was a very nice boy," says Mary.
"Handsome too. Nice smile. So polite.
He seemed very smart."

"And here's the weird part," I say.
"His cousin was Vinnie Green."

Mom and Dad are blown away
like me.
Mom's all, "That's cray-cray."
Dad's all, "There are no coincidences, I suppose."
Lenny's all, "Does he know that Vinnie's funeral was
here?"

My eye brims with one tear.

"Yep. And here's the thing:
Vinnie Green was an organ donor."

It gets all *Twilight Zone* in the room.
Mom bites her lip.
Dad takes a sip of water.
Lenny stares.

He says what we are all thinking
without even blinking.

"What if you have Vinnie Green's heart?"

I look at them.
The room spins a little bit.
I am sinking.

"Well then," says Great-Aunt Mary.
"If Faith has that heart,
there will be
an incredible connection.

Like a thread
that can't be broken,
tying Faith to Vinnie Green's family
members.

Especially to this
Jimmy Winters,
who was Vinnie's best friend."

And then Lenny puts an end
to all the serious talk.

"Faithie has a boyfriend," he says again.
"Faithie and Jimmy sitting in a tree.
K-i-s-s-i-n-g ..."

I laugh.
Happy is the best way to be.

Sweating It

It's four thirty,
and my hair looks dirty.
I wash it again.
Dry it, straighten it, make it shine.

"Almost wine and dine time!" calls Mary
through the bathroom door.
She's hanging out.
She doesn't want to go home.
She obviously wants to see Jimmy again.

I can relate.

Is this a date?

Extra deodorant.
Makeup.
Hair straightened.
Check.
My face is a wreck.
Two zits.
That's the pits.

Oh, snap.

What the crap
should I wear?

Hiking, dinner.
What would Jimmy Winters like?

I finally decide
on a denim and lace
black sundress
with my best red
Dr. Martens boots.

You can't be a failure
if you're wearing your
Docs. You wouldn't catch
me dead in Crocs.

"I think I nailed it," I say to myself.
I take my deodorant from the shelf
and give it another swipe.

I'm
sweating
already.

He

is

here!

I
go
down
the
stairs
and
there
he
is.
I
feel
like
Cinderella.

Is

this

my

prince?

If the Shoe Fits

"Hey," he says.
"Hey," I say.

"You look cute," says Mary.
"I love your boots."

And then
we all
notice
at once:

        Jimmy Winters and I
        are
        wearing
        the
        exact
        same
        red
        Docs!

My heart tick-
tocks.

"What did you expect?" Jimmy says.
"Doc Martens are too cool."

We put our four feet together,
lined up, matching, and Mom
snaps a picture on her phone.

"I'm posting this on Facebook," Mom says.
"Caption: Birds of a feather flock together."

"Funny, honey," says Dad.
"Too cute," says Great-Aunt Mary.

"Faithie and Jimmy
sitting in a tree,"
says Lenny.

I shush him.
"Hush!"
I blush.
My face
matches our
boots.

"What a hoot!"
Mom says.

"You two are too
cute," Mary says.

Seat Belts Are Not Optional

Jimmy's car is a
VW Beetle, blue.
"I call it Slug," Jimmy says
as we get in.
"It doesn't know how to move!"

"It's cool," I say,
and then I apologize
for my entire
family.

"I'm sorry for my brother.
      I'm sorry for my mother.
I'm sorry for my weird dad
      and my quirky great-aunt."

"Your family seems very
cool," says Jimmy. "Don't worry.
I like them."

"Awesome.
They do grow on you
with time."

"It's not a crime
to love your family.
I do. I love mine.
I hope you do
too."

My heart skips a beat.
Or two
Or three.

I'm going to meet his family?

Sweet.

"And by the way," Jimmy says.
"Buckle up, please. I like when
people stay alive.
Seat belts are not optional
when you ride
with me.

Sweet.

His Music

Jimmy Winters's car
actually has
an eight-track!
One of those
music players that
take those old
eight-track tapes.

He plays classic
music: Zeppelin and Pink Floyd,
the Doors and the Stones.
He plays all the songs I love!

His favorite Floyd song is
"Wish You Were Here," and his
favorite Stones oldie
is "Wild Horses."
And he loves
"Knocking on
Heaven's Door."

We are riding in a car,
but I feel like I could
soar.

I
could
fly.

I
could
die
from
happiness.

A Moment to Remember

"So do you know
that eight-tracks
were how people
listened to music,
like in between
vinyl albums
and cassettes?"
Jimmy says.

I just nod.
My body
is full
of the music
and the putt-putts
of the Bug Slug.
And I just know
that this is a moment
to remember
forever.

He pulls into a driveway.
We are at Jimmy's house.
It's a cute little white cottage
with blue trim,
like the opposite
of a funeral home.

"Nice," I say. "I like those yellow flowers.
And the white wooden fence."

"My mom says fences and flowers
make a house a home," Jimmy states.

I smile.
"I already like your mom," I say.

"Look," Jimmy says.
He points at a window.
"They're waiting."

Three faces are at the window.

"They can't wait to meet you," Jimmy says.

We go inside.
A gray cat runs to hide.

"I made a pie!" says a lady wearing white.
"Hi. I'm Jimmy's mom, Elizabeth."

She's pretty.
She has Jimmy's eyes.

"And I'm the stepdad Brad," says a man.
He shakes my hand.

"An honor to meet you," he says.

Another lady
who looks like
Jimmy's mom
lifts her eyes
to mine.

"Hi," she says. "My name's Kate.
I'm Elizabeth's sister,
Jimmy's aunt.
And Vinnie Green
was
my son."

"That's why
you look familiar,"
I say to Kate.
"We met."

"I don't remember
much of the service,"
Kate says.
"I was out of my head
with stress
and
grief."

I get that.
"I'm so sorry
about your son.
I heard Vinnie
was such
a nice guy."

"He was,"
says Vinnie's mom.

          "He was a wonderful son."

I nod.
Smile.
Take a big breath.
I'm not that great
when it comes to
talking about death.

"So, Faith, we debated
whether to send a text
or to call you with this news.
But we decided
that an in-person meeting
was the best
thing to do."
Jimmy's aunt takes a big breath.

"Here's the thing, Faith.
We asked to be told
about who Vinnie's
organs went to.

It might seem like
a weird thing to do.
But it gives us comfort.

And, Faith, honey …
Vinnie's heart lives on
in you."

The air in the room
becomes full—too full—
with emotion.

My heart—
that new heart
that came to me—
beats and beats,
so hard,
like a star
about to explode.

"Vinnie was
your donor, Faith,"
says Kate.
"You have
his heart."

I'm Kind of Dizzy

They tell me to sit a bit
to absorb it,
to let it sink in.

"It's a shock,"
says Jimmy's mom.

"You need
to give it a minute
to process."

Kate sits
on one side of me,
Jimmy
on the other,
as I fall onto a sofa,
letting it take me in,
taking this news
into my head.

I am holding hands
with a lady named Kate,
whose son
is dead.
Kate
lays
her
head
against
my
chest,
and
she
rests
there
for
a
long
time
hearing
the
sound
of
the
heart
that
kept
her
son
alive.

The
heart
that's
now
mine.

Thank You

I say to Kate,
"Thank You
for telling me
this news.
And thank you
for giving me
this gift.
Thank you
for the heart.
Thank you
for allowing me
to have a part
of Vinnie.
Thank you
for keeping me
alive."

There's lots of crying.

Jimmy sits by my side
the whole time.
He's not scared off by
the feelings.
He's good at dealing
with me.

After we've talked and cried,

cried and talked,
it's time for me and Jimmy
to take a walk.

"We're just going down the path
through the woods," he says.
"To that old abandoned foundation
of the never-finished house
I told you about."

We go outside

into sunshine.

It's bright
in my eyes.

"I haven't cried
like that
in a long time.
I bet I look
like a wreck."

"You look great,"
Jimmy says. "Perfect."

He reaches out
and brushes my cheek,
rubbing gently.

"Except for this eyeliner
that was crying too," he says.

I like the feel of his hand
against
my
face.

His cousin's heart
is starting
to race.

Fairy Tale

We walk
through green leaves
and trees,
an enchanted forest
path that's like a trail
to a fairy tale.

Sticks and twigs
crunch
beneath our feet.
And Jimmy Winters
lifts
a hanging branch
away from
my face.

"Almost there," he says.

"I'm liking this trail," I say.

"Me too," he says.

"Especially the part
about being with you."

This really does feel
like a fairy tale.
And this magical trail
leads me
to my
happily ever after.

Alone

"Here it is," Jimmy says.
"My favorite place."

We are there.
It's an old stone foundation.
Crumbly.
Just the bottom floor
of a house

                    that never was.

"It's just so quiet
and kind of
sad," Jimmy adds.
"But it also has
this vibe
of tragic magic.
It reminds
me of things
that are possible.
And how everything
needs to begin
and end
somewhere."

The foundation is cool,
but better yet is being with Jimmy.

We are the only ones in these woods.
The only ones on this path.

We
are
all
alone.

We sit side by side
on the old stone wall,
feet swinging in the air.

Our matching boots
look
really
cool,
like we are a
private army
of just us two.

"Smile," Jimmy says.
He holds out his phone.
"Selfie."

Jimmy clicks a picture.
We look at it.

Our faces actually look great
together.

Behind us is a white orb,
      like feathers
            on the wings
                  of an angel.

"Check it out," Jimmy says.
"There's nothing behind us.
So what
could it be?"

I shiver.

"It's Vinnie,"
says Jimmy.

The sun is setting,
and the last rays
are splayed through
the leaves on the trees,
radiating
in a circle
around Jimmy's face.

"Now you look
like an angel,"
I say.
"You have
a halo."

"Heck, no," says Jimmy.
"I'm no angel."

"You seem
pretty perfect
to me."

Nobody speaks.
Not me.
Not him.
On a whim
I touch
my index finger
to his.
Just for a minute,
skin
to
skin.

I can't tell where
I begin.

Dusk

We are still sitting
on the foundation.
It feels like
summer vacation.

Now there is just
a slight shimmer of moon.
Fireflies flicker too.

A few stars sparkle.
It is getting dark.

"Well, it must be
time for dinner,"
says Jimmy.
"We'd better get back.
My mom will have
a hissy fit
if we don't eat."

"Yeah," I say.
"She made a pie!
What kind?"

"I have no clue,"
Jimmy says.
"But I'm sure
it will be
delicious.
And you can have it
with ice cream,
if you like."

His eyes meet mine.
His hair is covering one eye.
I want to reach out and
brush it back, but
I'm too shy.

I really,
really
like
this guy.

Ticktock

"Can I just feel it?
Just for a minute?" Jimmy asks.

"Um, what?"

"Your ... heart.
Can I just feel it beat?"

I nod.

"Sweet," Jimmy says.
He carefully
and lightly places
his hand
on my
upper chest.

His palm is
soft
against the place
where my heart—
Vinnie's heart, *our* heart—
keeps the pace.

"It keeps
the beat
of me," I say.
"And it works
great."

"I feel it," Jimmy whispers.
"I can feel it."

I try
to smile.
I can feel it too.

Vinnie Green's
heart
is beating hard.
Faith Hope Stevens's
heart is beating hard.

I look up
into the sky.
I find
a star.

Thank you,
I say inside my heart.
Thank you, I say
to that star.

Lights

"Let's get going,"
says Jimmy Winters.
"It's not far."

As we walk
through the dark,
I see the lights
of Jimmy's house
shining up ahead.

They beckon
us.

The lights
guide
us
through
the
darkness.

Wishes

Somehow
my wishes
are coming true.
I have a boy
like Jimmy Winters
by my side
and a heart
like Ringo Starr
too.

Sometimes
life
can be better
than new.

Sometimes
a girl is so happy
she doesn't know
what to do.

Sometimes
a fence is painted
just the right
color of white,
and a little house
is trimmed in
the exact right
shade of blue.

"I have no clue
how I found you,"
Jimmy says.

"Dude," I say.
"We found
each other."

"With a little help
from our friends,"
Jimmy says.

We start to sing
old Beatles songs
together.
Our harmony
couldn't be better.

We sing
"With a Little Help
from My Friends"
and "Hey Jude"
and
"All You Need Is Love"
and
"I Want to Hold
Your Hand."

I am off the hook
with joy.
I love hanging
out with this
boy.

This is better
than Disney.
I feel all fizzy.
I am a princess,
and this
is
my
prince.

The shoe fits!

Wow

Jimmy entwines   his fingers   with mine.

Wow. Just. Wow.

I feel

fine.

The nighttime air smells like lilacs
                and something warm and sweet.

"I am so ready   to eat," Jimmy says.

"I can't wait   for that pie," I say.

Inside and Outside

Of

the

heart

that's

now

mine

beats

inside …

The stars shine.

The moon smiles.

And my heart

beats   hard

All

the

while.

Want to Keep Reading? ...

Turn the page for a sneak peek at another book from the Gravel Road Verse series: Linda Oatman High's *Teeny Little Grief Machines*.

ISBN: 978-1-62250-883-9

Ticking ... Tocking

My name is Lexi
     (rhymes with sexy)
McLeen, sixteen,
     and this is what I

believe:

     we are each

Teeny Little
     Grief Machines ...

ticking ...
tocking ...

bombs
programmed to explode ...

if we have not

already

detonated.

MY ENTIRE FAMILY IS A DISEASE

Dad: Alcoholic. Depressive.
Borderline Personality Disorder.

Stepmom: Anorexic. Anger Issues. Bipolar.

The two of them together:
hoarders of cigarettes
and lottery tickets
that never win.

Blaine: Autistic. ADHD.

And me:
artistic.

That's what *they* say
anyway.

I paint
in shades
of blue.

The poetry
is just so

     I

          don't

               explode.

ONCE I CARVED H-A-T-E
ON MY ARM

With scissors.

Just the tip.

Skimming.

Slicing lightly.

A tiny silver nip
of skin.

They thought

I must be a

cutter,

but I wasn't.

There was no knife.

I just
hated
my
life.

IT ALL STARTED

After we lost
the Baby.

It wasn't our fault.
Carissa,
my little sister,

just died in her white crib
in my bedroom
one night.

Peacefully, in her sleep, all tucked in,
bundled, swaddled, surrounded by pink
princess bumper pads and soft fuzzy blankets.
She wasn't on her stomach.

I can still see her face, sweet,
pink-cheeked,
eyes closed, baby butterflied eyelashes like
tiny splayed paintbrushes wisping her face.
She wasn't breathing. I checked for breath.

Linda Oatman High

Linda Oatman High is an author, a playwright, and a journalist who lives in Lancaster County, Pennsylvania. She holds an MFA in writing from Vermont College and presents writing workshops and assemblies for all ages. In England in 2012, Linda was honored with the *Sunday Times* EFG Short Story Award shortlist. Her books have won many awards and honors. Information on her work may be found online at www.lindaoatmanhigh.com.